Published by: Next Foundation Press

Text & Cover Design by: Melissa King

Edits by: Nicci Rosengarten

Illustrations by: Ricardo Ayala

ISBN-13: 978-0-9965687-6-0

The Writer and the Snowman: A Story About Purpose

Dr. John A. King

The Writer
and
the Snowman

A STORY ABOUT PURPOSE

a short story by:
DR. JOHN A. KING

DEDICATION

To those that have IT, celebrate it.

To those who've lost IT, seek it.

To those who've yet to find IT, pursue it.

Mr. Joyce

As the sun peeked through the trees and over the recently cleared couch, Mr. Joyce stretched, yawned, and meticulously combed his whiskers.

Slinking onto the floor, he meandered over to the curtains and reached as high as he could, rhythmically clawing them open, allowing the sun to splash on the old oak floorboards.

It had been an interesting 8 days, he thought, as he circled himself onto his favorite spot in the middle of the doorway to the kitchen.

Mr. Joyce reflected that once again, The Publisher had made the right decision sending his writers up to see him. Some had creative difficulties, some needed inspiration, but all could benefit from his wisdom and life lessons.

Laying on the warm floor, watching his tail flick in that disembodied cat sort of way, he thought long and hard about these different groups of writers and concluded that the significant difference between them was their disposition toward naps.

The therapeutic nature of a good nap is tragically overlooked, he thought to himself. Take for example this latest chap The Publisher had sent out here to the cabin. This particular Writer had, in fact, been one of his most challenging cases to date. He was a man who, when it all started, was obviously well-versed in cussing, stomping, drinking and smoking cigars, but who knew absolutely NOTHING about napping. The man couldn't sit still for ten minutes, let alone recline in repose for a brief intermission.

At the mere thought of napping, Mr. Joyce stretched with delight and recalled that up until two days ago, he thought he would lose The Writer to the black pit of depression he seemed to have committed himself to, but then Bernard, faithful old, somewhat misguided Bernard, had come up with a plan. This plan ended up nudging The Writer into a fresh start and a new direction.

A jolly good show all round, he thought.

His reverie was interrupted by the hostile appearance of a dust mite, stirred up by The Writer as he walked around whistling to himself, while preparing breakfast for them both.

As the Writer settled down at his desk and started to click-clack away, Mr. Joyce let himself out of the cabin and onto the deck. As he leapt up onto the deck railing, Bernard turned to him and said, "Will you look at that, Mr. Joyce! A smile. Who would have imagined that Frosty would get himself a smile? Just goes to show you, you never know how it will end. Mr. Joyce, I may really have to rethink this whole 42 thing."

Looking down with great affection at the smile on the face of the all-but-melted Frosty, Mr. Joyce added, "See you next winter old bean. Well played."

frosty

Day 8

As Frosty laid there, he replayed it all, recalling and savoring his final moments, trying to hold on to it all through his slowly dripping mind.

He thought about the first round warming thing he had ever seen.

The first cat he met, (which, incidentally, also involved the first conversation he ever had), the first time he started to wonder what it was all about, and the first time he smiled.

Day 4

Well he didn't actually have a conversation, because he couldn't talk—no mouth, you see. And as far as hearing, he wasn't too sure how that happened, either, because he completely lacked ears. All he knew is that as he watched

Mr. Joyce and Bernard the squirrel sitting on the porch railing, he just sort of knew what they were discussing.

Bernard was going over the fact that he was absolutely, positively, without a doubt, and completely, emphatically sure that 42 was the answer to the ultimate question of life, the universe, and everything—that it was the "it" they all came looking for at the cabin. (One night while he was watching through the window, very small people on a screen had said it was so, so it must be. Small things are very clever, he assured Mr. Joyce.)

*On this particular morning, a most peculiar thing happened. It was one of those things that at the time was very small, but at the end of it all, changed everything, like throwing a pebble in a pond.

---

*This is the point where if Frosty knew what a pebble and a pond were, he would look back and say, "On this particular morning, a most peculiar thing happened. It was one of those things that at the time was so very small, but at the end of it all changed everything, like throwing a pebble in a pond." But he didn't, so he couldn't, but the bloody author insisted on leaving it here, meaningful metaphor and all that sort of writerly crap—self-important twat. (-Editor)

Frosty had just been standing where he had always stood, wondering what it would be like to have legs, and trying oh so terribly hard to not listen to Mr. Joyce and Bernard, while at the same time hearing everything that they were saying.

At just that moment, HE stomped out onto the deck and started kicking the post, yelling, "I've lost it. I've lost it!" Then HE made large circular motions with his arms, "What is the meaning of all of this?!?"

HE then kicked the post one more time before hopping up and down on one leg, screaming, "FAAAARCCCKAARRR THAT HURTS!!" and heading back inside.

Now while all of this had been going on, Bernard had scurried up a tree while Mr. Joyce had sat, flicking his tail, ignoring the ruckus.

Hopping down on to Frosty's shoulder, Bernard said, "Quite strange don't you think? Been going on for quite a few days now."

"Ahhrrghh," yelled Frosty.

"What's wrong?" he asked.

"Ahhrrgghhhhh," he yelled again.

"That's what you said the first time. It's really not a polite answer, you know."

"You scared me."

"Sorry about that."

"You can hear me?"

"Of course I can."

"Where are you?"

"On your shoulder."

"My What? I can't see you. It would be best if you go sit where I can see you."

From the railing, Mr. Joyce called, "I think he would prefer you back over here with me, dear fellow, he can't turn his head."

"Is that so?" Bernard chattered.

"Yes, yes I would, actually," stammered the snowman in a very perplexed tone (in so far as a snowman can have a perplexed tone).

As Bernard scampered back to the railing, Mr. Joyce said in a cat-knows-best sort of way, "I think that days like today, yet again, prove my point."

"How so?" inquired Bernard.

Looking over the serene forest with its fresh dusting of snow he continued, "Your theory, dear friend. The 42 theory. Something as beautiful and wondrous as all of this could not possibly be reduced to something as quantifiable as a number. And what about the poor chap inside? His angst, his search, his pain—surely you would have to agree that he is searching for more than simply the sum of the first six positive even numbers? My friend, when people like that come here, they are trying to find their IT."

After about three minutes of listening to their banter, Frosty couldn't contain himself any more. "What's an 'IT'?!?" he blurted.

"Ah, my dear Frosty. How good of you to join in—that, my dear friend, is the question for all the ages. IT is different for everyone. IT is the thing that adds the warmth to mornings, and the soft glow to our evenings. IT is the very thing we were created to do. IT is the thing that gives all of this wilderness its majesty and this madness called life its meaning. IT is the thing that most people spend their lives trying to find, instead of simply enjoying IT."

As he turned toward the window, his voice softened to a purr of concern, "IT is what our dear friend the Writer here has lost, and I am fearful that if he doesn't rediscover his IT in the next few days, things could get rather tragic."

"Mr. Joyce, I'm not sure I understand," said Frosty.

"Ah...well you see my dear new friend, that is the question that he and his lot are preoccupied with. Where to start... hmmm, you see, that fellow there is known as a Writer. Now, Writers are a peculiar bunch. They tend to be somewhat prickly and self-absorbed, which always amused me, because they are so terribly self-aware of the fact that they are. You see, most of them end up chasing themselves around in circles endlessly, a little bit like Old Hank next door; chasing his tail, around and around, and never get any closer to it...madness really."

"What's a HANK?" said Frosty, as soon as Mr. Joyce took a breath.

"A what? A Hank, oh, that's Miss Gladys' dog, the lady next door. No, she isn't a dog. You don't see her chasing her tail, do you? Hank is the dog. He is that large, distasteful... ungraceful, noisy..."

Bernard broke into Mr. Joyce's ravings, saying, "Now, now, Mr. Joyce, don't get worked up. We really must press on and discuss The Plan with Frosty."

Staring back in the window, tilting his head ever so slightly, Mr. Joyce continued, "Ah yes, Writers. Well there are many types of Writers, but basically they do the same three things: they are the Recorders of Legends, Tellers of Stories, and the Compass of Truth."

"That sounds very impressive," Frosty responded.

"They seem to think so," Mr. Joyce said, watching intently.

Distracted by movement inside the cabin, Bernard whispered, "I do believe he is doing it again, Mr. Joyce."

Sighing, Mr. Joyce said, "I believe you are right, Bernard. We have so much to do and so little time."

As Frosty looked past them, he noticed that the writer was sitting at his desk, staring intently at something. Sometimes he would hold it to his chest, sometimes he would cry and yell at it, but most of the time he would just talk to it.

"What is that thing he is holding?" Frosty asked.

"I know, I know, I know!" Bernard said excitedly, "I think that is his IT. Yes, that's what I think it is. It's his IT."

Turning from the window, Mr. Joyce looked kindly at his friend, "Bernard, I am sure he believes it was for a while. Frosty, that is what the Writer's kind calls a memory."

"A MEMORY?" Frosty responded.

"A memory," echoed Bernard. "It's a thing what was, that isn't anymore until you think about it again, and then it is a thing that is."

"Very good, Bernard," stated Mr. Joyce admiringly. "There are good memories, bad memories, happy memories, sad memories, old memories, and new memories." He continued, "Let me give you an example: every morning The Writer walks out that door and he is carrying a big old mug. And that big old mug is filled with—"

"Ahh that's good," blurted Bernard.

"Yes that's correct, Bernard, it's filled to the top with Ahh that's good."

"Or Oh that tastes like CRAP," Bernard quipped.

"Yes, my dear friend, that is the other name for what goes in there. Now Frosty, if someone walks out on the deck with a cup of Ahh that's good, they sit there relaxed, smiling and talking to me and Bernard. If, however, it is filled with Oh that tastes like CRAP, they generally screw up their face, throw it at Bernard, and shuffle back inside to try again."

"They really don't mean to throw it at me," Bernard added, "it's just that sometimes I am in the bushes checking for nuts."

Unperturbed, Mr. Joyce continued, "Imagine that we are all like those big old mugs they carry around. And memories are what are inside those mugs. Good memories make you want to sit outside and smile at the world. Bad memories make you screw up your face and throw it at Bernard and stomp off."

"I'm not really following," Frosty responded, wishing he could crinkle his forehead or rub his brow.

Bernard responded, "The problem we have here is that every morning this Writer comes out, tastes what's in his mug and goes, 'Oh that tastes like CRAP,' and never throws it away! He just sits there drinking it, looking miserable, and being sad and lonely. He only ever gets up to go and get another cup of Oh that tastes like CRAP, which he then also drinks."

Frosty said, "To be honest, it sounds a bit silly. Why doesn't he just throw it at you?"

"Some of them find that very hard to do. It's like they acquire a taste for it, or don't know how to fill their mug with anything different."

And here is where the ripples started. Thinking out loud, Frosty said, "Then why don't we help him try and find something new? Maybe we can help him find his 'Ahh that's good?'"

Smiling silently at the perplexed snowman, Mr. Joyce jumped down from the railing and padded toward the door, saying, "That, my dear friend, is precisely what we need to talk to you about tomorrow."

"Oh," Frosty replied.

While he reached up to get a firm grip on the fly wire door he said, "And Frosty,"

"Yes?"

"Those twinkly things you see up there, they are stars, and the big one is Mrs. Moon. You should try to listen to them sometime. They have been wondering why you are not talking back."

Before he could ask any more, Mr. Joyce started to claw at the screen and very firmly, but politely meow, "Good fellow, would you please get off your duff and open the door for me."

This was met with a loud noise from inside the cabin, lots of thumping, and finally, a "Hurry up." Mr. Joyce, unflustered by the Writer's urgency, slowly ambled through the door and headed for his couch.

Day 7

Brief though it had been, he felt he had lived his life fully. Complete was the word he thought best to describe his life. You see, by the very nature of their creation, his kind, by and large, were not given to existential contemplation. When your average lifespan was between 20 minutes and

2 weeks, and entirely out of your control, you didn't waste a lot of time doing what Mr. Joyce said the Writer did a lot of, which was apparently gazing at his navel.

Once Mr. Joyce explained to him what a navel was, he found it quite strange. The Writer hadn't given him a navel, and even if he had, he could hardly gaze at it, could he? Unless of course, his head fell off. Which was strangely what he found himself able to do right now.

When he realized what a navel was, he was rather pleased that he had not spent a minute of the previous 6 days wondering if he had one or even wondering what it looked like or what it was for.

As Mr. Sun started to disappear, the soft and quiet stillness slowly started to fall. Frosty loved this time. So quiet, yet loud with new and exciting sounds and creatures.

Every day, the stillness went from oranges and yellows to the softest of black filled all the way up with stars and Mrs. Moon. On this night, they looked so totally different. He wasn't straining to see them through the trees as he had before. He was lying there looking straight up at them, and they were wonderful. They seemed to be dancing and singing.

Suddenly, in a very soft kind of way, Frosty started to hear what the stars were twinkling at him.

"Hi.   We see you.   Hi.   Hello.
Hi.   I can see you.
             Hello there!   Hi.   Can you see me?
   Hi.   Hi!   We see you.
             We see you.   Hi. Hi. Hi. Hi.
                  Hi!
      Hi.   Hi.

                          How are you?

      We see you.

                          No, over here, me!"

Then all of a sudden, the wind stopped blowing, the trees stopped dancing, and the stars were all quiet, except for the largest one of all. She said in a silky warm tone, "We love you. We love watching you. Mr. Sun and I are so proud of you. You make us all so happy."

And then suddenly, the trees started dancing again, clapping their leaves and the stars started singing, "So happy! So happy! Amazing! Yes, thank you for you! We love you. You're wonderful! Thank you for being you!"

At that moment, something indescribable started to fill Frosty's round, remote chest. He would have muttered: Oh, it is wonderful. Oh, it is wonderful! over and over again if he had a mouth, but didn't, so instead, he thought it so hard that it actually started to make him feel warm inside.

"Oh, it is glorious. Oh, it is glorious!" Frosty thought as loud as he could.

"I found IT. I found IT."

"Oh yes. Oh yes!" he thought over and over and over and over again till the birds started to join in as Mr. Sun danced back across the sky, glowing bright with approval.

It was so simple once he saw IT. It was his IT. It had been here all the time.

IT was his, and he could give IT to everyone who wanted IT.

I made the Writer laugh.

I made the blackness smile.

The stars are happy and the trees clapped their hands, and Mr. Sun and Mrs. Moon love me, just me.

It all makes me warm inside. This is IT, I found IT.

And as he laid there, something happened for the first time in his quiet short, cold and very uneventful life, he started to smile.

the Writer

#1 Blank Paper

He had been sitting now for days...

(Brooding
Staring
Cussing
Blubbering
Wandering
Waiting
Wishing
Hoping
Yelling
Screaming
Railing
Fuming)

             ...despondently.

"A billion emails a day," he muttered as he looked at her photo on his desk.

These idiots. Formulated opinions, researched and recorded at the speed of thought. No depth, no quest, no reason, outside the desire to add their shallow musings to the white noise of a mind-numbed and dumber generation. "WIKI-BLOODY-PEDIA IS NOT THE FOUNTAIN OF ALL TRUTH!!! You morons."

"Have all the great words been written, all the grand stories told?" he sullenly asked her.

The ever-increasing mound of dirty dishes seemed to spill out of the sink in an attempt to march to their freedom across every horizontal surface, like a Dean Koontz version of The Sorcerer's Apprentice.

"Little cabin in the bloody woods," he thought, "tree hugging, lame arse BULLSHIT. Whose bright idea was this? Probably your mother's."

Through the window, The Writer noticed the snowman he built relentlessly staring back at him. Sliding his feet into the greying Winnie-the-Pooh slippers she had given him, he muttered, "Fuck off, Frosty," as he shuffled over the eternal stretch of worn rug to the fireplace that was "all the fucking way over there."

Next to the fireplace sat a basket of goodies that The Publisher had arranged to have delivered on the first day he had arrived. The envelope was the only thing he had opened. The handmade card sat on the mantle amongst an array of meaningless odds and ends left by previous occupants.

He picked it up and traced his finger around the hand-painted daffodil, marveling at how similar it was to the one he had carried everywhere with him these last few years. The only difference was that his had the addition of "I love you, P.B.," and a fading outline of her bright red lipstick kiss.

Opening it, he read the words one more time:

> "I know this is hard and thank you for trying.
>
> We both love you very much.
>
> We pray you will take this time to find your feet and your voice again.
>
> She would want that, and the rest of us need it."

Get away. Find your voice again.

Doubling over, he screamed, "WHAT DOES THAT EVEN MEAN?!?!?" Unfortunately, this very loud display of emotion happened right over the top of a bulging ashtray of cigar stubs and pipe droppings.

The consequence was immediate, and no amount of running around, worrying his hair or pulling his ears, saying, "Oh bother!" was going to stop the Krakatoa-like cigar ash cloud from descending on the only clean chair in the cabin, which also happened to be occupied by Mr. Joyce at the time.

Mr. Joyce stood, stretched, disinterestedly shook himself, and headed off in search of the least-soiled article of clothing on which to continue his nap, paying no heed to the Writer's spiteful glare.

"Bloody cat," he muttered as he dusted off the front of his last cleanish T-shirt (if a 3-day-old-soy-sauce-stained Foo Fighters shirt could be called clean) and set off in search for his pipe and tobacco, repeatedly muttering, "Why me?" followed by his other well-rehearsed mantra of, "What is the point of it all?"

Eggs Hemingway

After about an hour, The Writer returned to the lounge room, clutching the stem of his pipe fearful that it would run off and hide someplace more obscure than the spoon drawer in which he had found it.

Approving of his timing, Mr. Joyce stretched, yawned and adjusted his whiskers, all under the disbelieving gaze of the Writer.

"How could Mr. Joyce so effortlessly ignore me?" The Writer wondered to himself.

Having arranged himself for his mid-morning frolictation, Mr. Joyce stretched purposefully and with a single, protracted "Meow" commanded that all attention be on him.

Standing there watching him, The Writer said, "You are utterly heartless. You show nothing but disregard for my struggle. Don't you know what is at stake here? If I don't come up with something they like, I AM DOOMED. A failure. Cast aside. Ruined. I will literally become like those books on the discount table in some second hand shop."

As if in response, Mr. Joyce meowed one more time in summons, and padded down the hallway to wait insistently at the back door.

With a loud sigh, resigning to the demands of His Royal Highness, The Writer headed to his bedroom and then the bathroom in search of his winter long johns. He eventually found them in the kitchen under two empty pizza boxes he couldn't remember ordering, and a drained bottle of cheap whiskey that probably accounted for: 1. why he couldn't remember ordering or eating the pizzas, and 2. his headache and his increasingly dim view of, well, everything.

As he hopped from one leg to another trying to put his pants on, he caught his painful big toe on the material. Cussing loudly, he promised no one in particular that he wouldn't kick the deck rail or anything else ever again.

Passing the full length mirror in the hallway, he said in Mr. Joyce's general direction—although not for his exclusive attention, that would have been a waste of time, "I feel and look more like Cousin Eddie in National Lampoon's Christmas Vacation than Earnest Hemingway in a Moveable Feast. I know Hemingway experienced writer's block, but I wonder how he kept eggs out of his beard?"

Pipe in hand, he poured himself a cup of I Wonder if This Will Taste Any Good, and followed Mr. Joyce into the cold, knowing full well he was about to have a miserable time, and he just needed to get it over with so he could come back inside and continue his pathetic existence.

The Reason

Swaying slightly on the porch swing, grimacing at his coffee, The Writer watched the old Black Forrest cuckoo clock methodically go through its paces. He decided he hated that as well. It just hung there, ticky-tocking towards its hourly destiny. It never rushed. It never stalled. It never wondered what its purpose was or what the next bloody book was supposed to be about. In 2-1/2 minutes it was going to send that stupid little bird out and make its stupid little sound and shatter the only peaceful part of The Writer's perfectly horrible morning, day, year, life.

While looking at his bruised, ugly toe, he prayed silent prayers calling for the untimely death and destruction of the offending timepiece. He was interrupted by a seemingly inconsequential event that, some three years later, halfway through a TED Talk in front of 2000 people, on a Thursday, he would realize was THE event that propelled him from the national to international stage as an author.

The audience knew nothing of this at the time, they just wondered why he seemed to lose his place and then randomly blurted out "I'll be buggered," followed by "I'm so sorry Mr. Joyce, I should have been nicer," before continuing his presentation on "How I Overcame Writer's Block through Reconnecting with Nature."

Mr. Joyce, however, was not concerned with the reaction of any TED Talk audience now or in three years time. He was occupied with far more important matters like how to get from here to there without getting his paws wet. Perched on the porch railing, staring out over his domain, he was contemplating a snow-laden branch about 2' away. He decided that it did indeed look stable enough and that if he was to jump on it, it would hold his weight. He could then proceed to gracefully shimmy down the trunk to inspect the garden gnomes without having to tippy toe through the snow.

It all happened in slow motion at the speed of cat.

As The Writer started to turn to preemptively deliver his morning tirade to the cuckoo clock, Mr. Joyce launched himself from the railing to the limb. The extra weight took the branch down and at just enough of an angle so that the snow on the branch moved ever so slightly. Momentarily, Mr. Joyce appeared to do something he rarely did, which was to reconsider the wisdom of his decision. Once the branch stopped bobbing, he proceeded with unruffled calm in the direction of the trunk.

In his telling of the tale, Mr. Joyce clearly and emphatically states that all that happened next was as he planned and had discussed with Bernard the night before and that at no point does he look like a drunken college student on a treadmill in a Youtube video.

From where The Writer sat, it looked spectacular.

Mr. Joyce, feeling his snowy footing start to move, commenced to run for all nine of his lives. His little black paws were pumping at full leopard when the branch, finding release from its icy burden, hit him in the belly, cat-apulting him in a perfect arc that resulted with him flying straight into Frosty's head knocking it onto the ground and leaving him perched on what was now its headless shoulders. Not one to be caught off guard, Mr. Joyce composed himself, circled once and settled down to lick his paws only stopping to look disdainfully at the owner of the noise coming from the deck as if to say: "What are you laughing at? Of course, I planned it."

On the porch deck, The Writer stared in slack-jawed disbelief, the only sound being the clamber of pipe and a low "You have got to be shitting me," which was immediately followed by uncontrollable howling and laughter. Initially the sound startled him. It had been a long time since he laughed, but then with a sense of relief he found himself giving in to it, enjoying it, slouching in to it like one does into a favorite sofa.

About two minutes into rolling around the deck, he wiped the tears from his eyes just long enough to check on Mr. Joyce, before falling back on the deck childishly shrieking.

As he recovered his composure, The Writer knew there was only one appropriate way to respond to the spectacle. He stripped butt-naked and launched a flying rugby tackle in the direction of Mr. Joyce and Frosty.

As he lay there face-first in the snow, he became aware of three things:

1. He had missed Frosty altogether—he hadn't even made it half way.

2. He could feel his testicles recede into his body... no seriously, he could. It was otherworldly.

3. Mr. Joyce's small feet stepping gingerly over his bare butt as he headed to the deck, completely dry.

Slowly rolling over, he sat up and was struck by how beautiful the day was. Mr. Joyce on the other hand, sat at the back door impatiently waiting for his doorman. The furless one for some reason had looked in his direction and started rolling around in the snow again, bellowing and laughing and crying.

"Ridiculous," Mr. Joyce thought and went back to straightening his whiskers. "Writers."

Clean Canvas

He had risen early the next day, 9am, (well that was early compared to the years of stumbling out of bed between 11 and 2, after going to bed between 3 and 6), and decided that he would do something different—take a walk.

Later that afternoon, he waved goodbye as Bert, from Ethel & Bert's Country Diner, pulled out of the drive way. He reached down, trying to stretch his back and touch his toes, sighing to himself as he grunted to get past his knees. "Maybe next time I decide to break my exercise drought I won't do it with a 5 mile walk to lunch," he said to himself as he hobbled inside to pour a whiskey and run a bath—in that order.

Sitting in the now-tepid bath, cigar-smoked to the nub, The Writer pondered the events that had led up to his today.

When all of this had started for him, it had been simple, clean, pure, fun and funny. His last book had launched him. They said he "came from nowhere," a "nobody," who was now an "overnight success."

They said he was the greatest, the best, the freshest, the newest, blah, blah, blah. After the incident happened, they stopped calling, caring or even remembering. The bastards just moved on and told him that for the good of his art he should as well. They couldn't possibly understand that she had been his art.

Climbing out from the bath, he recalled their first meeting.

Before it all took off, he hadn't cared what others thought. In the beginning, he never wrote for money or fame—none of that had been important.

He had started to write because he needed to share those ideas and pictures with anyone who would hear them and see them. He just wanted to put his voice on paper.

Moving to the kitchen, tired but invigorated, he noticed Mr. Joyce turning endless circles on his lightly ashed chair. He realized he had more in common with the cat than he did with the stable of writers at the big publishing houses, who seemed more committed to prostituting their gifts than writing with passion and purpose. Mr. Joyce ran, jumped, played and embraced all of life, its risks and rewards, for an audience of one — that is why he always landed on his feet—because they were HIS feet.

The following day, after letting Mr. Joyce back in, "That cat sure is regular," He gave himself completely to the task at hand. Over the next 8 hours, order returned to the cabin and his mind as he tamed pile after pile of dirty dishes and unwashed clothes, sifting through the emotions and events that had led to this point, stopping sometimes to sigh, sometimes to cry, but each time feeling somehow cleaner.

As he vacuumed the rug and swept the floor, The Writer realized that he couldn't think any clearer today than he did yesterday, but that wasn't important. What was important is that he could feel clearer and that, he realized, had been what he was missing.

He stood, looking out at the woods, seeing them as if for the first time, fresh and full of possibilities, no longer stifling and restrictive. Gazing casually out at Frosty, he laughed, he couldn't remember putting a smile on his face, but he was glad he had.

Fresh coffee in hand, The Writer looked down at the pad, and for the first time in years, the paper didn't scream at him to perform. Instead, he saw a blank canvas inviting him to create, to tell a story because that was the thing he realized he had been born to do.

As he settled into his chair, Mr. Joyce rubbed against his leg and purred victoriously. Picking him up and scratching the little cat spot between his ears, he looked at the woman in the photo, while muttering to the cat, "How about we write her a chapter and then you and I have a little nap after lunch?"

Picking up her photo, he tenderly kissed it, saying, "I miss you, baby. I love you. It might take me a little while, but I'm going to be okay now. I promise."

the Publisher

Jerry Maguire

The Publisher sat in the corner booth gazing out the window nursing his whiskey. Looking around the pub, he wished it were the 90s so he could smoke. Land of the Free, Home of the Nanny State he said to himself patting the pocket where two of his finest hand-rolled organic cigars were wrestling to be free. If things go well with him, maybe later tonight, at home, Janet would love that.

The first winter sludge was playing havoc with traffic so he assumed he might have a while to wait, time to gather his thoughts.

This was a good, warm place...a natural choice for them to meet again, back where it all began 10 years ago.

He fondly remembered their first accidental encounter while diving for lobsters in Florida. It had been a good season, and the conversation had started around their shared passion for SCUBA diving. He had invited the young man, back to the bar, and over the course of the evening they had ended up swapping life stories and shared dreams with ease, the way men do with strangers.

The usual tang of the Reef Cup turned bitter on his palette while he sat listening. The light of the young man's passion had caused the realization of his cynicism to cast a shadow over his normally carefree spirit. He had given the last 30 years to helping folks turn their hobbies into art only to watch them trade their soul for the temporal baubles of fame and fortune, and he was burned out from it.

As he skewered the pineapple at the bottom of his glass, he wonder if this Kid was any different?

When he had started, he had seen himself as a publishing pirate, skull and crossbones corporate logo and all. He didn't have the biggest publishing house in the world; yet, on the street, it was known as one of the most influential.

His approach had been simple: no 5-year self-perpetuating creatively castrating contract; just a handshake; shared costs; and shared rewards. If a writer didn't make it, The Publisher just gave the book back and said, "Good luck." The result of this approach was that every writer in his stable was an international bestseller making more money in a month than many others did in a year.

That, however, was years ago. Success put him in the crosshairs of the disenfranchised wannabes that he had cut loose. Every false accusation under the sun from racism to sexual harassment forced him to hire more lawyers than editors, put contracts in place, and hire so-called talent managers to distance himself from the very artists he desired to help.

But the Kid had been different. As they sat at the bar that night long ago and shared their plans for the upcoming year, the young man talked with passion about a book he was writing. It was more than a book; it was a mission, a one-man mission to inspire people toward greatness, to live beyond their past and grab hold of their future.

As they sipped the hours away, The Publisher found himself coming alive, stirred, not by the young man's talent or gift, as he hadn't seen any of his work yet, but by the raw passion that emanated in his words. The thing that forced The Publisher's hand was a casual comment the Kid made: "I want to help people find freedom, kind of like Black Sam Bellamy, the pirate…have you ever heard of him?"

Looking at him with different eyes, The Publisher answered in a forced, casual manner, "I have. I know the story well."

"You have?" the young man exclaimed in disbelief, "THAT'S GREAT, hardly anyone has…I want to be like him. I hate the way society has robbed people of hope, and I want this story to…"

As the evening closed out, The Publisher wrote his office number on a napkin and said, "I might know someone who could help you. Call me if you're really interested in pursuing your dream. This is my direct line."

A week later while staring melancholily out his window, his secretary buzzed through a call:

"There is a very flustered young man, who I can't understand on the phone. He is speaking very fast about lobster, Florida, pirates, paper napkins and washing machines."

"Thanks, Janet, I wondered if I would hear from him again," he said. He thought the "young man" was probably in his early thirties.

Picking up the call he said, "This is he."

"I'm sorry, I lost the napkin but I remembered your name, I google'd you, I couldn't find it, you publish books, well, actually I didn't lose the napkin, I washed it and then it was all wadded up, you're the pirate guy, I love what you stand for and I'm sorry I would have called earlier, but I couldn't read the numbers so well, I washed the napkin, have you ever done that?"

Leaning back in his chair, slowly smiling to himself, The Publisher thought: "I might like this kid, if I can just get him to slow down and shut up."

"So, if I have got this correctly, you washed the napkin, but you'd be interested in meeting with me?"

"Well, yes, that's what happened, and yes, please, that would be awesome, I can come today, well not today because it's late and you're probably really busy, but I'm not, no, I'm just sitting here"

"Where?"

"...at the hotel. I flew in this morning and can come by whenever you'd like. I mean, I'm not stalking you...I just thought if I were here you might have time. And if you did, well, I would already be here, you see?"

He thought about saying, "I think that was some sort of record for speaking without breathing," but instead asked, "Where are you staying?"

"I'm sitting here at some hotel they should rename The Cockroach Inn, it's out by the airport, but that doesn't matter, I can get a ride."

Unable to contain himself any longer, The Publisher laughed out loud and said, "I like you kid. Cockroach Inn eh? Stayed in those plenty of times in my life. Why don't you pack up your stuff and meet me at Barney's. It's a little Irish pub on 7th in say two hours? We will have a chat, and then you can come back to my place, we have a spare room, or I will put you in the Westin for the evening. How does that sound?"

The Kid said, "That would be great. Thank you so much. I'm kind of glad now that my credit card bounced. That sounds way nicer than sleeping in the foyer," and hung up.

The Publisher was sitting there shaking his head and grinning when Janet walked towards him and said, "I haven't heard you laugh like that in forever. You should do it more often, it suits you."

Rising to greet her, he took her in his arms and said, "Can I move our movie and pizza date to tomorrow night? I'm having drinks with that crazy kid at 7 o'clock."

Putting her hands on her hips, in her best matriarchal tone, she said, "As long as you promise me one thing."

"What's that?" he asked quizzically.

"You have been a little distant since Florida—unsettled, restless. Normally, I don't mind, but I have just scheduled the painters for next week so any new life up-heaving adventures are going to have to wait. So, you're not allowed to go all Jerry Maguire on me again. Agreed?"

Straightening to attention, he placed his hand on his heart and pledged not to go 'Jerry' on her.

Shooing him out the door with a smack on the bum she said, "And hug Hadley for me."

Another

The soft rolling Irish accent of the waitress broke through his reverie, "Another?"

Looking up he asked, "What other whiskeys would you suggest?"

"Didn't you like the Teeling?"

"Yes I did, thank you, great suggestion. I was just wondering if you had anything else I might try?"

"Hmmm," she said, assessing him as if she were unraveling a great mystery. "You don't strike me as a Jameson guy; personally I think it's overrated. Used to be good before they started buying up all the real distilleries, but don't get me started on that. Dingle is all the rage, and we have that. People also seem to like Dead Rabbit and Templar Bar."

"Lots of choices, what is your favorite?"

"Here's the thing. I believe that good whiskey is like art. You like what you like and that is it. No point in pretending and just going with the crowd. That's just what they do with all the ooooing and ahhing at a Jackson Pollock or that shite by Barnett Newman.

Have you seen it? Onement VI?

Total bollocks. I don't know what goes on in some folks' noodle. But they should call it Two Blue Squares and pay someone to hide the fecking thing.

As I was sayin', just because someone told you that you should like it, doesn't mean ya have to. Now me, I'm from Kilkenny, God's own country it is, and as far as art goes, I like a bit of Tridu Doyle and Val Bryne. There I have said it. That is just the way it is so you can like it or lump it, I'll not be bothered.

Now a good whiskey is the same. Me you ask? Well, my favorite is Writer's Tears with three drops of water no more. You Americans want to throw a handful of ice in there, or ruin it completely with carbonated rubbish. To me, that is like taking a Raphael painting and turning it into a join-the-dots coloring book."

Unsure of what had just happened, he raised both hands and said, "What is your name, young lady?"

"Why?"

"I would just like to know to whom I am conceding defeat."

"Emer. E-M-E-R. Emer."

"Well Emer, I surrender. I am waiting for a friend, so make it two Writer's Tears with water on the side please."

"Good," was all she replied before striding victoriously towards the bar.

The Meeting

The one-eyed god of doom and gloom sat overlooking the crowd running its commentary of disasters and terrorism across the bottom of its screen at a mesmerizing pace. The press of bodies and the cries of relief filled the space, people turned and welcomed friends and strangers alike into the steamy sanctuary, collectively choosing to ignore what the talking head was screaming at them.

No longer was this place merely filled with the soggy-seeking refuge and respite; they were now adventurers who had made it safely across the vast unknown of 7th and into the sanctuary of Barney's Island.

A stockbroker who from 9-5 sounded like an Oxford dictionary yelled, "There's a good girl, Emer, would you turn that crap off or give us the footy? We don't need to see anymore shite from those bastards for the day." This was followed by a bar-wide collective shout of agreement.

Considering the crowd anew, The Publisher silently grinned in amazement. People were always so ready to embrace and drown in stories of fear instead of hope; horror instead of happiness, giving greater commitment to worrying about tomorrow instead of loving and living today. But for a moment this merry band of urban refugees seemed to have climbed to a higher plane than usual, and he loved it.

This near undefinable attitude was the very thing that had struck him about the young man when they first met. The

Kid was different, naïve…no that was unfair…un-jaded was more fitting, or maybe dreamily preoccupied was a better description. He was always trying to put words to things he saw that others didn't seem to value anymore, like hope, joy, new, present.

Right at this table 10 years ago, the kid had walked in and before they even sat down, he had started talking about his novel, going over character development and twisting plot lines. A mop of hair bobbing excitedly over some 400 pages of single-spaced manuscript covered with first, second and third edits written in a form of hieroglyphic scribble a philologist would struggle to decipher.

As he sat, not so much listening but rather feeling what the young man was saying, when a familiar touch broke the moment. "Hi Daddy, Mom called and said you were coming down with a new friend."

"This is the young man I mentioned. The one I met in Florida a couple weeks ago."

"Hi new friend, I'm Hadley," she said, smiling at the young man who was just staring at her with big eyes, cheeks slightly glowing while he makes a bubbling throat-clearing sort of sound.

"Wow, this is only the second time I have seen him take a breath," said The Publisher.

Teasingly she ask "Can he talk?

As if on cue, the young man jumped to his feet, extended his hand saying, "Yes I can," followed by, "Oh bother!" as he noticed he had bumped the table and spilt water all over his notes.

As he raced to stem the flood, she couldn't help but laugh ever so sweetly and commented, "He sounds like an A.A. Milne character. I'll get a cloth."

"Don't worry, I've got it, thank you," he said dabbing vigorously with a second napkin. "See, it's all cleaned up. Not to worry. And yes, I do speak, see and I can write also!"

"I'm glad." she smiled

"So am I. You're beautiful. Oh, I just said that out loud didn't I."

To which father and daughter both laughed and said in unison: "Yes you did!"

Which was met with a second "Oh bother", and a "I do that sometimes."

Hadley kissed her father again and teasingly said, "I'll get that cloth and come back with fresh water. Why don't you work out what Pooh Bear here wants for dinner."

Through two bourbons and a BLT he listened as the young writer talked over his plate of Jalapeño poppers and onion rings, none of which where eaten, but did in fact come in handy to illustrate a point or two.

Two hours later, as he was trying to herd him towards the car, his phone dinged with a message:

"Hey Jerry,

I hadn't heard from you, so I went and made up the guest bedroom.

Does this young man have a name or am I supposed to just call him The Kid?

Please tell Hadley her dinner is in the oven.

And don't YOU make plans tomorrow. I have some for us. And you better not come home with a fish in a plastic bag." ❤️ 🐓 😍

The following morning over breakfast, The Publisher realized that what he saw in the young Writer wasn't just talent, but something else, something simpler: he just loved to tell a story. Between simultaneous swallows of coffee and bagel The Writer randomly mused, "I believe a good book, be it a sci-fi or biography, must be like a movie for my mind, yet instructional for my soul. I want it to not only take me somewhere, but also move me somewhere."

The following week he flew back in for what was supposed to be a weekend and ended up being a month of rewriting, re-editing and reheating half cups of coffee for the umpteenth time...all set to the soundtrack of classic Chicago blues. The result was the final draft of what would become an instant National bestseller.

All of the Tomorrows

Dropping the young man at the airport had been bittersweet. All the way home he had stared unfocused out the window as she drove. He realized he hadn't felt this way in a long time about a writer or a project and wasn't quite sure what to do with this new/old emotion.

Later that evening he stoked the fire pit and settled into his favorite chair on the back deck. Janet sat quietly snuggled in beside him watching the flames dance and waiting for him to talk.

Leaning forward and poking around the fire, he muttered more to himself than anyone, "He has no idea what is coming. I hope we don't lose him."

"You mean you hope he doesn't lose himself," she responded.

"Well, you know what I mean."

"I do," she replied stroking the back of his hand. "You mean you hope it all doesn't go to his head like it did for Russell and Debbie. You mean you hope he doesn't get jaded and affected by the corporate politics like you did. You mean you hope you can protect and save him from himself. Well, you can't. But what you can do is give that young man something no one else will ever give him. That is friendship without an agenda and honesty when he needs it and doesn't want it, and a place to belong. Because that is what he needs more than anything."

He turned to her marveling at her intuition, gratefully kissing her cheek, "I don't know how to ever say thank you for marrying me."

"Well, you can start with a glass of wine and a dance. Followed by some crappy pizza from Angelo's and making out on the couch now that Hadley is out for the evening and we FINALLY have the house to ourselves."

Grinning he replied, "How about we start with making out and then I make us pizza while you drink wine and pick out the movie?"

Jumping up she started walking quickly towards the house, calling out over her shoulder, "First one naked wins," to which Hadley exclaimed from the kitchen: "I heard that! I haven't left yet!"

"Then you better leave soon," her mother called back. "Things are about to get noisy!"

"MOM!!!"

To Pirates

"Anyone sitting here?" said a familiar voice

Still looking at the table he replied "I am saving it for an old friend. He is running a bit late, weather and all."

Lifting the glass to his nose, the new arrival asked, "What's he drinking?"

"Whatever the waitress tells him he is."

"A bit like that is she?"

"You have no idea."

"Good to see you, Dad."

"Good to be seen, Son."

As the waitress approached, he knocked back the whiskey, held out the glass saying, "Can we have another round, please? This one seems empty."

"Yes you can. But that is NOT the way to drink a fine whiskey. Ainmhí." she said turning back towards the bar muttering something in Celtic they were certain was not flattering.

"If that was her, I see what you mean," The Writer said while removing his coat and settling in.

"It was indeed," The Publisher replied.

They sat quietly and comfortably as the cloak of familiarity settled in around them.

Trying to keep his voice steady, The Writer turned to the older man said, "Thank you."

"What for?"

"For making me go."

Quizzically he responded, "It was your TED Talk. I didn't do anything."

"Not that. To the cabin."

"Oh. That. Well, that was a miracle. I thought I was going to have to hog tie you and drag your sorry ass up that mountain."

Emer suddenly appeared, deposited the golden liquid and gave a well-rehearsed recital on the correct way to appreciate Irish Whiskey. It was delivered in such a tone and way that it elicited a 'yes ma'am' and a shared grin as she was absorbed back into the fray.

Reflectively The Writer said, "We should have done this sooner."

"That would have been nice."

"Yeah, well, I was being a dick."

The Publisher didn't say anything , he just nodded once in agreement, like only the closest of friends can do.

"I deserved that."

"I didn't say anything..

"You didn't have to."

Over the years, their business relationship turned into a friendship that few people ever experience. What started as give-and-take had morphed into a give-and-give as the young man's dedication and passion for his craft combined with The Publisher's skill and wisdom skyrocketed him to heights that many dreamed of and few obtained.

Along the way, The Writer had fallen passionately in love with the girl that would keep him centered and focused throughout the fame of that first novel. She stewarded the royalties and saved all she could, even taking the odd shift at Barney's when he was out of town. Many wondered why she didn't buy more stuff or do more things, but she had been around the business and the people in it for so long that she knew success was seasonal. Hadley wanted them to learn from others mistakes, not mirror them.

Sipping their drinks in unison, The Writer said, "She's right, it's better done this way."

"She's clever. Probably the most cultured waitress I have ever met in this place, except for one," The Publisher said.

And there it was.

The specter, looming.

The thing to be talked about.

The Writer felt the cold fingers of loss start to crawl across his soul, dragging with it the sadness that always locked down his mind, paralyzing his emotions and words.

He took out the old greeting card from his coat. It was battered and worn. The Writer laid it on the table and traced with his finger the words and daffodil that had faded in all but memory, like everything else about her.

"I miss her."

"We all do."

"How is Mom?"

"She's really proud of you Kid, and she desperately wants to see you."

"I was wondering, well I was thinking, that if you didn't mind and you didn't have plans that maybe I could stay with you guys if it is not too much of a bother and all."

Keeping his voice level, The Publisher started to get to his to his feet, "I'll call her and let her know we are coming home."

Putting his hand on his arm he asked "Dad, can we wait a bit, just sit a little longer, maybe talk some more?"

"Sure we can Kid, sure we can."

Over coffee and a cheese plate, The Publisher offhandedly said, "We didn't think you would make it."

"Neither did I. I was either going to come back from the cabin with an outline or not at all."

"Mom worried about that."

"After the incident, I just couldn't do it anymore. The crowds, the book tours, the TV appearances, the shallow concern and comments from strangers angling for an autograph. And every time I went to write, I wanted to ask her what she thought of my work, or where I should take it; but, she wasn't there. I miss my wife, Dad, I miss my Hadley."

Pulling his chair closer, he put his arm around his shoulder and said, "We all do Son, that will never change. But we are also very, very grateful that we still have you. it was not your fault that you lived."

And it happened.

Safe in her father's arms, the thawing of the frozen sadness around his heart broke like a dam and the flood of despair and grief erupted and washed down his cheeks and over the card his wife had made for him for their anniversary all those years ago. And for just a moment the faint outline of 'I love you, P.B.' caught their eyes and they sat there with wonder as their mourning turned to joy.

Standing to his feet The Publisher said:

"Its time for our toast. We haven't said it since she died, but tonight is the night we celebrate her."

At the top of his voice and to the surprise of the bar, the distinguished grey-haired gentleman roared, "QUIET EVERYONE, QUIET PLEASE!"

"Today is a special day, a day I have hoped for a prayed for and cried for many years. A day of healing, a day of hope. Emer, I would like 4 bottles of Writer's Tears on the bar and shot glasses for everyone, please."

After the initial excitement the crowd settled, looking at the pair expectantly.

"Today my son came home and I would like us all toast his return.

Now this is a special toast, a family toast.

A toast written by my Hadley, that's right my Hadley, the girl whose picture sits right there on this wall. It's called the Pirate Toast."

Facing each other the two men men roared as one with all the grief and joy that was in them:

> May the storms of life be few
>
> May your love be one and true
>
> Like an anchor hold you firm
>
> And like a compass lead you home
>
> TO PIRATES!

In unison the bar erupted with the cry of 'To Pirates' as bottles where passed and songs of love and loss filled the air with joy and memories, as only Irish folk songs can.

Hugging his neck and kissing his brow, The Publisher said, "She would be proud of you, Son."

"I hope so," The Writer responded.

"I know my baby girl. I know so."

"Well, I am going to take a leak and call Janet to tell her you're coming home,"

"Tell her not to make up a bed, I'll sleep on the couch."

"Bullshit!" the older man yelled over his shoulder. "She's had the guest room made up for 5 years now. You will sleep where you are told."

As they arrived at their cars, his father-in-law asked, "What happened at the cabin that turned it around for you?"

Stopping in his tracks, he said, "I only figured that out today. So there I was, in front of 2000 people when I remembered something that happened while I was out there. I was having a particularly difficult time when I first arrived, so I built a snowman. Then, a couple of days later, that old mouser of a cat you use to have up there, Mr. Joyce, well he and I believe a squirrel, were involved in all of this and well...you see what happened is I think it smiled, no I am serious, I think the snowman smiled at me..."

Unable to contain himself, The Publisher roared with laughter and started waving his hands around saying, "Stop. Stop." Finally, he stammered, "Stop right there, buster. You need to save this till we get home. Janet will kill us both if she misses out on this one. A cat, a squirrel and a smiling Snowman...this we have got to hear."

ARTISTS/CONTRIBUTORS

Dr. John A. King, Author

I love to write. I enjoy the process of taking a concept and making it attainable and applicable. I also enjoy it as an excuse to sit in my garage by myself and smoke cigars.

Melissa King, Contributor, Layout Designer

Many artists down through history talk of a "muse" that propelled them to greatness--complex, fun loving, inspiring. I have the privilege of having breakfast with mine daily.

Nicci Rosengarten, Editor

From hip hop to diva 90's record label PR expert, Nicci has not only been a great blessing but an awesome friend. Her editorial contribution was vital to the success of this project.

Ricardo Ayala, Artist

Ricardo brought Frosty and Mr. Joyce to life for us. We couldn't have done this project without him.

To see more of Ricardo's amazing work, find him (like I did) on IG @unoriginal_doodler.

Also by Dr. John A. King

This book shares John's gritty process of rebuilding his life after the onset of Complex Post Traumatic Stress. On his journey, you'll find practical tools, unlikely mentors and his trademark Aussie sarcasm. #dealwithit is the perfect book for anyone who is getting up to go again, or is in the middle of the fight and just needs to hear, "You can make it."

Visit drjohnaking.com/shop to purchase.

No Working Title: a Life in Progress is a collection of poetry, writings, stories and art that deal with the taboo topic of the effects of sexual abuse and pornography on boys as they grow into men.

**This is an adult book that deals with adult concepts in adult language.

Visit drjohnaking.com/shop to purchase.

NO WORKING TITLE
— A LIFE IN PROGRESS —

by Dr. John A. King

Exploring the effects of sexual abuse and pornography on boys as they grow to manhood.

From Me to You

poems about love and other shit.

Dr. John A. King

COMING SOON!

Poems about life and love from John to his wife, Melissa.

Visit drjohnaking.com/shop to purchase.

www.ingramcontent.com/pod-product-compliance
Lightning Source LLC
Chambersburg PA
CBHW081157170626
46813CB00009B/3226